Anne

An imagining of the life of Anne Frank

Story by
Marjorie Agosín
Wellesley College

Translated by Jacqueline Nanfito

Illustrated by
Francisca Yáñez

Solis Press

On Saturday, July 15, 1944, Anne Frank wrote in her diary:
I still believe that people are truly good at heart.

© Marjorie Agosín 2017

First published in Spanish in 2015 by Das Kapital Ediciones, Santiago, Chile

ISBN: 978-1-910146-26-2

Published by Solis Press, PO Box 482, Tunbridge Wells TN2 9QT, Kent, England

Web: www.solispress.com | *Twitter*: @SolisPress

About this Book

When I was twelve years old, my grandfather, Joseph Halpern, gave me a copy of *The Diary of Anne Frank* as well as a diary for me so that I could start my own. These gifts from my grandfather inspired my work as both a writer and a defender of human rights.

My copy of Anne Frank's diary was bound in beautiful green velvet, which reminded me of my grandfather's deep and kindly gaze, as well as the color of the forests of southern Chile that was my home. Anne's words have always held so much meaning for me. I could see, smell, and touch everything that she experienced and, more than anything, I felt her zest for life. The presence of Anne Frank has accompanied me ever since: Her imagination and, above all, her great desire to be a writer. However, Anne's life, along with those of six million others, was tragically cut short.

The "Final Solution," the name given to the Nazi plan to exterminate all the Jews in Europe, leaves a dark stain on the history of the twentieth century. Cruelty and dispassionate killing, along with the burning of books and the destruction of culture, were the legacy of the Nazis. However, they could not silence all the voices, those of Primo Lévi, Charlotte Delbo, and many others remained, but it was always the voice of Anne Frank that spoke to me.

This book is specially written for children. I want the memory of Anne to remain, although not for her to be remembered solely as the most famous victim of the Holocaust, but as a wonderful young writer of the time. I want her to be remembered as a young teenager who loved to play, to eat ice cream, write poems, talk to trees, and fall in love; in short, someone who embraced all the wonders of life.

Marjorie Agosín

Above the city of Amsterdam in the country of the Netherlands, the rain filters through the vermilion and ocher trees. The raindrops feel like beads from a broken necklace of colors. Here the rain is so different from the drops that fell upon me in Germany. Everything glistens in this city. Amsterdam is tiny—Mother says—like my grandmother's thimble. One day Mama will come to know the maze of canals that seem to sing so sweetly. The two of us will go arm in arm along the streets, calling out their names in this new language. Here, everything is different and I am not afraid of anything.

Mama always says that I should do more embroidery, sewing, or mending, so I say to her: "Mama, caring for the words that I write is like embroidering stories." She laughs but Mama is always filled with sorrow. I call this sorrow nostalgia.

Margot is my sister. Together we stroll through the city where the canals seem to be in conversation with each other. Here the wind is gentle and the rustle of the leaves fills my head. Petals tumble from the flowers and fall upon the water. Many people wander along the waterways and I hear the musical sounds of their elegant steps. Margot and I laugh among the canals.

It grows dark slowly and I like to imagine that I can touch the stars. The stars soften in the night sky, they flicker and don't seem so far away. Perhaps all of the beautiful things like water and laughter are within our reach. Even those who have left this earth through the tunnel of death may come close, merely by us chanting their names.

Here in Amsterdam, no one hurries. Here no one points at us, like they did in Germany, just for being Jewish girls. At times I ask myself, what is all this fuss about being a Jew?

"It is to be different," Papa tells us.

And so on Fridays, when the afternoon light fades slowly to allow the night to approach and the first star of the Sabbath appears, I know that I am entering a sacred time. Mama prepares a lovely meal and spreads out the white tablecloth embroidered by my grandmother. The challah bread is shaped like a golden braid. A sacred goblet is set to bless the wine. But what I like the most is the soup made of chicken broth with matzah balls and purple cabbage. The Sabbath is like a pause in the busy week for all of us. It is a time to give thanks for the fruits and flavors of the earth above all else. It is a time to be still and converse with God.

In Amsterdam we keep the same traditions that we celebrated in Germany. Visitors come to our house; it is customary on the Sabbath to welcome guests and make them feel at home.

Papa tells us that tolerance is part of being Jewish. We must learn to accept others and to accept those who do not think as we do. He always tells us that it is about learning to forgive those who don't understand and those who have a heart of stone.

I like it when Mama lights the candles. Her voice is soft and graceful when she prays in Hebrew. Suddenly I feel that the light of God graces our table with all of the light of the heavens and of the earth.

I like this city of Amsterdam. I learn its sounds and a new language. The streets are covered with cobblestones. Young girls, with blonde hair the color of wheat, wear white aprons that float and dance in the breeze. Although we are from another country, from another city, Margot and I feel at home. At the end of the day we all come from the earth, from the sun, from the sand, from the wind.

On Sundays we stroll through the open-air markets. The herrings hang from the ceilings of the stalls, these elongated fish with silvery iridescent sides, a deep-blue, metallic-hued back and a dreamy look.

In Amsterdam, it rains 175 days a year. There are something like 352 bridges, and I can't tell you how many canals, but I never tire of looking at them because everything changes according to the light. And in the distance there is the sound of the bicycles whirring along the narrow streets.

When we arrive home, Mama is always waiting behind the window. The window and she are inseparable. I love the color of the lace that graces the window frame, it is the delicate color of sepia, like the face of my grandmother, or like the color of sand, or of Margot's hair.

I remember very little of Germany. When I talk about it to my father, he tells me: "Anne, you must live in the present, that will help you to be happy. Enjoy the garden or a visit to the ice cream shop. The future will arrive soon enough and you have little power over it. Anne, don't think about the past, you must not allow life to pass you by."

I was born in Frankfurt in 1929. My family had lived in Germany for more than 200 years but suddenly we became strangers.

The German authorities introduced many laws against the Jews. First, they didn't allow us to eat ice cream in the streets. That was, indeed, tragic. Then, we could no longer go outside after eight o'clock in the evening, not even into the garden. Margot and I learned not to make a sound. We had to watch everything, the butterflies, the squirrels, the wind, through the closed window.

One day, the German authorities ordered that we wear the yellow star of David to show that we were Jewish. And that's how it all began. Papa told me how they had forced the neighbors to get down on their knees and clean the streets of Frankfurt. The strong acid made them ill. The people who make these rules are called Nazis.

The Nazis discuss what to do about the "Jewish problem," but we are not a problem, we are just people like them. Mama cried as she sewed the stars of David onto our coats. I found her tears among the stitches, but I left them there, so that they could dry in the sun.

My father, who sensed that there would be more trouble, sent us first to another city in Germany and then to Amsterdam. What is important is that we are safe and far from all of those rules and regulations, and that we always eat ice cream, that is what he told me.

I like to laugh, to play hide and seek with my sister, Margot, and I love to write. I don't know if I will be an actress or a writer. Writing gives me peace. I also like to imagine things that still haven't come to pass, but may happen in time.

For now, I want to become familiar with the canals of my new home, Amsterdam. A city full of aromatic rains, full of colorful houses that stand so close together that they seem to be embracing.

We arrived in Amsterdam when I was five years old. I began to make many, many friends and I so enjoy going out to play. There are children of all ages in the neighborhood.

Mama says that my favorite pastime is making mischief. I have three friends that I see day and night; well, not so much at night. As well as saying goodbye and telling one another that the angels will accompany us, we have also invented several whistles. A very sharp whistle is the signal to enter into the threshold of dreams. I have also taught them how to draw imaginary maps, with imaginary streets, with imaginary heavens.

In order to be a writer, one has to write and, more than anything, to play. Writing gives me peace and a strange joy as if the words and I were playing in a mysterious and secret place where many adventures happen. I often think about something strange: for example what would it be like to throw raindrops into my backpack? Or, better still, perhaps fill myself with fireflies.

My house is the color of vermilion and has some slender green stripes that separate us from our very quiet neighbors. These neighbors become angry when I sneeze; they don't like noise of any kind. Once again, rules! Once again, the silence in which Mama takes refuge, even though I don't think that it has to do with being Jewish. Margot tells me that I should learn to be less cheerful but that, indeed, proves to be impossible. I don't believe that they will ever prohibit me from laughing. I love to laugh, and to walk barefoot and to gather tulips that grow in the most inhospitable places.

I so like watching the light of the sky change when the herons fly past.

I so like seeing the changing colors of the leaves and listening to the sound of the bicycles as they glide by in the night.

The city wears the face of autumn and becomes the color of amber.

Of the many things that I like besides laughter, I can say that one of my favorites is the arrival of the fog over the water. It arrives quietly, like a guest that does not want to knock on any door, a guest that does not want to bother anyone, a guest that does not want to be noticed. But I notice. I sense it arrive and sail over the earth. I like the color of the fog, the color of history, with all its shades of gray. Perhaps the fog possesses the color of invisible things.

And then suddenly I ask: Why don't I receive letters from my grandmother? Has she been swallowed by the fog? Have they now banned Jews from writing letters? I dearly miss her postcards written in a language as elegant as she. But maybe they don't allow her to write in German.

Margot and I attend the Montessori school. We have bicycles that, like Mama says, don't seem to roll on the ground but rather fly over the cobblestones. They soar through the air, playing with the rain and the rhythms of the water.

I love my school and, above all, I love to talk. The teachers tell me: Anne, don't talk so much; Anne, listen; Anne, do your math homework.

Numbers escape me, they are so much above me, I believe that I can never find them, whereas, I devour words. I paint them with colors; they enchant me. I want to make earrings and necklaces out of them. I like all words and I like those that are simple, those that don't need any adornment, like the word "leaf," or like the word "dragonfly," or like the word "star."

The idea of being an actress now bores me, although having applause every night must be incredible. The best applause, though, is when I write a poem and read it aloud. Afterwards I give it to Papa and see the tears once again return to his eyes.

I will be a writer and invent great novels. I will write marvelous stories of love because, I imagine, to fall in love is to feel a slight tickle, perhaps like riding a bicycle accompanied by another, or like soaring through the sky without steps.

What interests me is to know important things. I ask myself does sadness have a color or can new words invent colors? I write down these thoughts:

1 What will I be, a journalist or a writer?

2 How does one stitch together a novel?

3 Who knits an enormous sweater and then brings its parts together?

4 Do tears have a color and what are they made of? One day I will perhaps take a photo of them.

5 If one cries while looking at the canals, will the tears be part blue or part green? Will the tears of autumn be amber, the color of the sun in the late afternoon?

One Friday evening as we prepare for the Sabbath, some friends of my parents come to the house. They, like us, lived in Germany, in the same city that we did. They felt that they were Germans too but, like us, they suffered under the Nazi laws. They only arrived in the Netherlands recently and it upsets them to talk about what they have seen, so we say that it is better to sing the songs of the Sabbath and to play chess.

Since it is Saturday and we don't have school, I will dedicate myself to inventing a stroll with my girlfriends through the center of the city.

Mama is waiting for us when we arrive home from school. Sometimes we see her half asleep, resting on the golden window that faces the Grand Canal. Her disheveled hair is the color of silver and seems to cling tight to the night. She waits for us with a smile that resembles a pale moon.

Each day I sense that she is more silent. It seems that she is becoming an expert in silence. "Mama, are you a professor of silence?" She laughs and she doesn't laugh. The truth is that I never know what she is thinking or perhaps she doesn't think and allows herself to be carried away by the melody of the days that are at once the same and always different. Her silence is like a thread tied to her lips. I don't want anything to tie me down, not even my shoes. More than anything, I want laughter to live inside of me and I want to ride my bicycle barefoot. That is what I want for the moment and it is in this moment where I most feel comfortable.

We have heard nothing from grandmother. We haven't received any letters, postcards, or news. It is as if even the earth has forgotten her.

On Saturday evenings I hear sweet sounds.

A distant piano.

The far off sound of a flute.

And with my hands I hold fast to the setting sun that gives me peace, helping me to embark on a journey towards sleep.

Sleep comes and goes like a boat that is adrift.

I hear the soft murmurs of Papa and Mama. They speak in Yiddish, the language of my grandmother.

I try to imagine stories in German, but this has become confused with the Dutch that I am now learning. I love this new language, the words sound as if they have emerged from the depths of the throat.

29-7 ———————

≡ 25-9 ——————

43-14-12 ——— 21-12 ———————

10-2 ——

20/10

— 10/1 —

3-12 —

20/10

At night, I imagine that I can hear the voice of my grandmother praying in Hebrew, a language that I only hear when the candelabras are lit at home and we sing. How I miss her, but I need only close my eyes to recall her fragrance and to see her face fresh from lavender and drops of speedwell.

As I peer out of the gilded-framed window, a light illuminates the whiteness of the snow, and in spite of the void left by those who are no longer with us, and in spite of the dark and somber voices of Mama and Papa from the next room, I am happy.

Tomorrow I will eat my favorite ice cream, strawberry, and walk through the city. Spring has arrived and my heart, like Amsterdam, is filled with tulips. I am so grateful for things, like the smell of springtime, for laughter, which is always contagious, and for being alive. I will become a professional in the art of giving thanks.

Margot and I walk to school together. At school we learn poetry, music, history, and sciences and they always ask me what my life was like in Germany. I only tell them the beautiful things, like the walks through the woods; I keep the things that I don't like to think about to myself in a very somber box. In the dark box of the memories that I wish to erase, I keep the remembrance of when the Nazis took away our rights to live, and on this I remain silent.

And would I have to pretend to be mute?

And would I love silence as much as I love words?

It doesn't matter. I will worry about those things later. Tomorrow is my birthday and I will dream about the presents that will appear at dawn. That's how Papa always does it, leaving the gifts hidden about the house.

The house is narrow and mysterious, but I always find my presents.

I was born on June 12th and today I am 13 years old. The day starts with rain, but it is only a light shower and soon it will clear up and the sun will arrive. How wonderful to have a birthday, it is like receiving the gift of life once again.

Mama doesn't like to invite many people to the house. She is more and more fearful and she trembles a lot. She says that only dear friends can come to visit: Papa's friends, those who work with him, a couple of neighbors, and I invite two of my girlfriends from school. They give me many presents, but what I like the most is the gift from Papa: It is a diary. The cover of the diary is made of red-and-white Scotch plaid fabric and it fastens with a very small, golden lock.

How lovely is the word "lock," it sounds crisp and clear, like the sound of a striking bell. It is a lock where I will keep only the secrets that resemble the color of violet.

My Diary

This diary is full of blank pages, a world yet to be conquered. I will fill it little by little with my secrets. At last, I will truly have a best friend, I will call my diary Kitty and write poems across the empty sheets.

I always write poems with my girlfriends from the neighborhood and we leave them in the mailboxes among the flowers, as if they were secret songs. I wonder whether to invite Papa to join in my game: He understands me.

I love Mama just as much as Papa but she is always telling me to do things: Anne, go straighten up your room; Anne, go help clean; Anne, be careful to not stain your dress; Anne, Anne, Anne! And so for that reason I will always seek refuge in Kitty. I might say: Kitty, let me tell you so many things. I know that the words listen to us. I know that the words soar and bring us stardust; they bring us the laughter of wayward angels.

Dear Kitty:

I feel that very soon I will embark on a long journey but it will be with you.

Dear Kitty:

I don't know why the sky awakens so very ominous. Might it be the bearer of other sorrows?

I love you,

Anne

A Day of Fog and Farewells

One day, my teacher at the Montessori school called to me.

"Anne, I have to speak with you after class."

"Have I misbehaved, Miss?"

"Of course not, Anne."

"What have I done, Miss? Have I been disobedient? Have I forgotten my homework?"

I approach her office and knock at the door. She calls me in and I look at her. She has very blue eyes, the color of the sailboats that enter the harbor at dawn.

"I would like to tell you something, Anne, which is very difficult. I am sure you know that the German Army has now invaded the Netherlands and we are under their laws; we are now an occupied country."

I am silent.

"Do you understand me, Anne? We are no longer free and cannot be the tolerant country that we have always been. Now, here in the Netherlands, we are filled with fear just like the Czechs, like the Polish, like so much of Europe."

She takes a deep breath.

"We have been told that Jewish students can no longer attend this school. They must go to the Jewish school; this will be your and Margot's last day here."

I see how the tears of my teacher fall slowly down her face, gray and blue tears. And my eyes also fill with tears, spilling like raindrops onto my cheeks.

"Also, Anne, I ask that, for your own safety, you don't say anything to anyone. Don't say goodbye to anyone. You must not trust anybody, not even me, my dear, sweet Anne."

We hug each other and tremble like those little paper boats that surface on the waves. I cry a lot, as if all of the water from Amsterdam's canals falls from my eyes … Then I tell her that we will see one another again because the heart will do everything possible to keep us together, and that I will always confide in her. My teacher shudders and I sense the dark shadow that surrounds us, a forewarning of the days of confinement ahead, days without laughter.

After class, around 3p.m., I leave the school. I don't have the strength to say goodbye to anyone. I don't even take my books or my notebooks. They already belong to the German Army.

Margot and I go home slowly, painfully. The bicycles no longer soar, they creak and whine. A gray fog hangs all around us. It enters my eyes, through my nose and mouth. It stays with me and paints me the color of sadness. I hope that perhaps one day we will return to the Montessori school and that the Netherlands will once again be a landscape of light, but at the same time, I am fearful.

In a secret chest, Mama keeps the Jewish star of David that I always used to wear around my neck. She says that I cannot put it on again yet. She doesn't want them to recognize us as Jews because the Nazis might mistreat or abuse us. I begin to understand that I should hide who I am and, more than anything, I should be suspicious of everyone. It all changes too quickly and I cannot understand anything or anyone. My parents seem suddenly to grow old and shrink in size. At times, I don't recognize them and I, myself, seem to be another person.

In the Netherlands now, we also have the 8p.m. curfew, we can no longer go out into the street or into the garden in the evening. How I would love to stroll up and down outside, to hear the sweet sound of the water and simply enjoy being in the city that is now my home. I long to laugh again, to lean out of the window, to dream about the arrival of autumn or spring and to imagine what wonders a new day will bring. I will not lose hope. I will not lose the color of beauty nor allow myself to take on the dark shades of pain. I will not think about malice.

Dear Kitty:

I am telling you that there are no bad people, that everyone is basically very, very good. With this I prepare to say farewell to our home. I have a feeling that better times will not arrive and that my father is preparing to take us on a journey to another place. I will no longer live in this colorful house …

Anne

The Time of Fear

I can only go out into the streets at certain times. But now, like in Germany before, we are supposed to wear the yellow star of David on our clothes. But Mama refuses to sew this on to my new coat. So I do it myself, taking great care with every stitch. I can only shop in businesses whose owners are Jews.

We have to put away my ping pong table. That is the only sport that I have enjoyed. I'm not very good at tennis, for example, but I am good at ping pong. Soon better times will come, Papa insists, indeed they will come. I can no longer find comfort in words or even in my dear Kitty. There is no freedom now, nowhere to go and no one to trust.

Life at home is becoming more hushed. I argue a lot with Mama. She always wants everything to be so neat and tidy, so disciplined. The Nazis are very orderly, they march along with their impeccable uniforms and huge boots. I hear their strides and am so afraid of them, but then I think: Their order is that of cruelty, why would we want order at home?

I find refuge in my room, which I painted all blue. Kitty accompanies me and I share everything with her. This is my sanctuary during these days of uncertainty.

The Nazi police have arrived with an order for Margot to present herself and be transferred to a forced labor camp. Papa's friends tell us rumors about what happens in these places. They say that the Nazis force the prisoners to work until they are dying and then they send them to camps where they are locked up and forced to breath in poisonous gas until it kills them. Such a thought terrifies me.

But perhaps during these days, death will be our most faithful friend, it will protect us from our pain and from the pain of others. More and more, my eyes are downcast. They now look like Mama's eyes and they have lost all their gleam. Even so, Papa still manages to smile. He invites his colleagues from work to visit and I sense that life continues.

From a very small window in the living room, I see my garden. Everything begins to wither there. I have named my flowers, but no longer does anyone visit them. I hug my diary, my precious Kitty, and I tell her, you will hold fast to all my words, those from the past as well as those yet to come. Oh Kitty, all I love so dearly is falling to pieces.

One morning, very early, so early that I confuse day with night and the whole world turns upside down, my father wakes me: "Anne, we have to leave, don't ask anything, don't say anything, don't speak, don't laugh, just follow me."

Every night my father puts my diary, my beloved Kitty, in his briefcase for safekeeping. I always trust him to look after it while I sleep. I feel too that Kitty, tired of so many words, deserves a rest. Papa also gathers the photographs of famous people that decorate the walls of my room. He carries all these things in his large briefcase.

Mama dresses me in layers of clothing: coats, sweaters, socks. It is the beginning of autumn but it seems that I am about to venture to the North Pole. She fills my pockets with food. I smile in silence as I imagine the fireflies sharing my pockets with cans of beans and fruit.

I don't know where we are going but I always liked surprises. Maybe we are setting off on a new adventure? Would we be alone on that journey?

Mama, Papa, Margot and I leave our home in Amsterdam at five in the morning. Everyone is in bed, even the waterfront is quiet and the sleepy cats lie in tight balls of fur. Not a single sound escapes our lips. The bicycles recline against the cobblestones as we bid them farewell and the chestnut tree sways in silence.

To my surprise, Miep from Papa's office is waiting for us with a smile that reminds me of a huge sunflower. She hands a bouquet of flowers to Mama, to Margot, and to me. Miep is Papa's assistant but she is also a friend. Moreover, she is my confidant and one day I will ask her about love and such things.

The Annex

Behind Papa's offices, there is a secret annex. Now I understand, we will hide there. We will all hide and weather the storm until it passes. Another family is with us, dear friends. We often spend the evening of the Sabbath with them.

I am afraid to reveal too much about this annex. I will only say that it is behind a wall of books and then there is a room where the brooms, dustpans, and dust mops are kept, and then another door, and then us.

There are rules in the annex. We cannot speak or even flush the toilet until after eight o'clock in the evening. No one can sneeze. We have to avoid suspicion.

Often I ask myself, what kind of insanity inhabits the minds of this world? Why should the Nazis have such a great hatred of the Jews? What have we done? Could we be so different from the other people? Papa says that the power in decline seeks out a scapegoat. Why separate ourselves? We are all just one family.

In the annex we have a lot of canned food, also figs and dried fruits and books, and I decorate my room with the photographs that Papa brought from my old room. I will make this room very beautiful, but it makes me so sad to always be in the darkness with enormous curtains. I wait for the night so that I can keep company with the stars. I will pass the time with Kitty and, indeed, I can become a writer.

From my window, I see a majestic tree. It is a marvelous tree and I would like to embrace it. There is also a clock that keeps time. All clocks are serious, like older gentlemen, but this one brings me peace. It makes me think that very soon we will leave this annex.

Here the hours are long, as if they don't have a beginning or an end. I have the time to imagine faces and think about my school friends. We left so quickly, we disappeared so suddenly … and I don't believe that anyone is looking for us, it is dangerous to hide Jews. Any citizen who dares to hide us would suffer certain death.

Over the months, I discover little things that make me happy. I read and read because the gracious Miep not only brings us exquisite jams, but also books, newspapers and my beloved magazines of movie stars.

I see the green leaves of the tree in front of my window and imagine them covering me while I sleep. I remember how naked it is in winter, and this makes me think of my own nudity. My body has changed and I am becoming a woman. It is pointless to wear pretty dresses in the annex, yet I still paint my lips at dusk.

I have become a very good friend of Peter, who is here with us. He is the son of another family. The two of us seek refuge in the attic of the annex where we can talk quietly, so quietly that it is as if our words fade and disappear, but we like to be there and feel a certain peace and stillness.

When there is a little bit of sun, I say to him, "Peter, we are at the beach. Let's dream that we are here on this marvelous beach."

I imagine the beach, splashing among the waves and, more than anything, being free. I imagine breathing the fresh air and wonder if the air is still free for Jews?

To help us through the monotony of the days, Miep brings us a small radio. At about nine o'clock, we congregate around it in order to hear what is happening beyond the walls of this annex. We know that the war continues, that the Nazis pay the Dutch to hand over Jews. We know that the Allied forces are advancing and that gives us strength to continue living. At times I still have a lot of faith and certainty that there are decent, honorable people in the world.

If I could recover the light of day.

If I could go out on my bike and laugh at any time.

If I could shout out loud my hopes of being a writer.

Then I would be even happier.

But in spite of it all, I feel free and a tiny hope sways throughout my body.

As time goes by I talk less and less to Papa and say nothing to Mama. She can no longer accuse me of being disorderly because I now share my room with a dentist—another arrival in our annex.

Here if we become sick, we cannot leave the annex. From reading so much in the dark, I need glasses, but they don't allow me to go see an optician. It would be too dangerous.

Perhaps what I like best is to be waiting for the tick tock, tick tock of the clock, imagining that the trains return with Jews who are alive and well, imagining that we will defeat the Nazis—and perhaps imagining that we will learn to forgive them.

They, too, are fathers, mothers, brothers, sisters, sons, daughters. They, too, know how to embrace their children.

What I most like is going to the attic with Peter. And, afterwards, in the evening, going down and joining the grown-ups to listen to the radio. The grown-ups seem to live in a separate world now. They live in search of certainties. Perhaps they think about their homes in the countries that no longer wanted them there and threw them out.

Papa has a map on the wall where he marks the defeats of the Nazis. I learn the names of the new towns and the new geographies. Papa's employees visit us often and this brings me great joy; the truth is that I tire of hearing the voices of the same people. A new voice is like being born anew. It is as if a bell has arrived to converse with us, we who are so isolated in this long seclusion.

They say that within two months the war will be over. I want to return to my Montessori school, to hug my teacher and study Greek mythology with her. The world opens up to me like an enormous mosaic every time I think about this. It gives me hope that one day we will leave this place and return to where we can feel the sunshine on our light-starved skin and hear the sound of the sweet, sonorous canals cascading over our bodies.

Over these last few days, we have been listening to the sound of hammering outside the secret door as Papa's colleagues build a shelf that holds heavy books. There are many informants in Amsterdam, and for very little money they will denounce hidden Jews. My father is always very cautious.

And if death were to enter by this secret door? And if they were to shave my head?

And if they were to give me soap in order to make me believe that they were taking me to the shower when it is really the shower of death? And if they were to make a bonfire to burn us? And if in an instant, they knock on the door, what would those hours be like? What would I be thinking about?

I am afraid but I make an effort to think that tomorrow is always another day. Tomorrow I will find bread on the table, Papa's smile, the magazines that Miep brings us, and the little pieces of sunshine through the partially closed window.

It is hard for me to read. I see very little. I can't imagine a life in an extermination camp, to do so is to imagine a constant death. Or perhaps death in those places is the best and the most benevolent out of all the possibilities?

And if suddenly they find us?

Mama, the watchful one, has our suitcases prepared.

What should I take to a concentration camp?

I won't need a comb because they will shave my head.

I won't need the photographs of my favorite actresses.

I will sleep in a bunk bed with other girls like me.

I won't be able to keep the photograph of my grandmother.

I won't be able to write love letters.

A25060

Lately I have been dreaming that they discover us,

That they come to search for us,

That they knock on the door several times,

That they ask Papa to accompany the police to the office of the *Gestapo*.

I have this dream every day.

I dream that they take away my diary, my Kitty,

That they shave my head,

That I have to wear a uniform with stripes

And that they cut Mama's hands

Then I can't find her.

When they arrive at these camps—and they say that there are several—

They separate the women from the men,

The children and the elderly.

The strong ones are sent into forced labor

The weak ones are given soap,

They are told that it will make them very clean,

But it's not true,

They take them to the gas chambers.

Might it be possible? But I write in my diary

And I write over and over again

"I still believe that people are good."

After ten at night, when all of my father's employees return to their homes, we hear on the small radio that the Allies are winning. Papa insists that in no time they will liberate us and the war will end very soon.

That makes me smile, that makes me dream. The first thing that I will do is strip away this golden star from my clothes and replace it with the beautiful one that I always wore around my neck, because it was my choice to wear it.

How I wish to be free, how I wish to breathe fresh air at any time, day or night. I will return to my garden and call out the names of the flowers. I will go and eat ice cream. I will write poems, but this time they will not be secret poems that might reveal so many things. I don't want to tell of the fear that I have felt here in this annex, but I do want to speak of my dreams, of the times that the sun, through that very tiny slit, embraced me. I just want to speak of lovely things …

Mama is always dejected, crestfallen. She has lost all her light. She has lost faith. When we prepare the candles on Saturday and pray in silence, not even then does she smile.

I always say to her:

"Mama, in spite of everything we are all together, you, Papa, Margot and I …"

"Yes, Anne," she repeats and kisses me on the forehead. But she says to me: "Don't forget that when they come to look for us, the suitcases will be ready with our belongings. If they find us and if we have to go."

It is difficult for me to enter into the realm of dreams. I ask the angels to watch over me. And then suddenly I fall asleep thinking that I hold the sun within my hands.

I have a feeling that they will discover us. Peter tells me that it is impossible, given that two years have passed, and that very soon we will be out strolling along the bridges of Amsterdam.

I'm going to turn 15, dear, dear diary.

Very early in the morning they knock at the door. They knock loudly and with fury. It is them. I look at my little suitcase near the door. Papa is studying Greek and Latin. I look at him as though I were saying goodbye to him. My diary is kept safely in his briefcase.

The door opens.
They have come searching for us.
Death has found us. Perhaps it will be our true refuge.
I don't think.
Mama hands me the blue suitcase that she always had ready for me and for Margot.

Farewell annex, farewell Kitty, farewell wind.
Farewell sun, farewell secret companions.

If only I could feel the hand of Papa and Mama.
The Nazis have enormous dark boots like a sinister night.
Mama walks first, followed by Margot, then me and Papa, bringing up the rear, always a gentleman.
We are going to an extermination camp.
What will they do with my hair?
Will someone say that, even though I am bald, I am beautiful?

One day will I find the hand of Mama and Papa. And will I be able to embroider words alongside Kitty?

Timeline of Events

1929   *June 12*: Anne Frank born in Frankfurt, Germany, to Otto and Edith Frank. She was the younger sister to Margot (born 1926)

1933   *January 30*: Hitler appointed chancellor of Germany

March 23: Nazi Party took full political control of parliament and government

Later that year, the Nazis began restrictions against Jews

April: Jewish businesses were boycotted

1934   The Frank family moved to Amsterdam in the Netherlands; Anne's grandmother remained in Germany

Otto began work as the director of a Dutch subsidiary of Opekta, a company that sold pectin and spices. The family found an apartment in Merwedeplein, in the south of Amsterdam

August 2: On the death of President Hindenburg, Hitler became *Führer*, the leader and dictator, of Germany

1935   *September 15*: the Nazis approved the Nuremberg Laws, which deprived German Jews of their citizenship, businesses, and a right to education

1938   *November 9/10*: the *Kristallnacht* ("the Night of Broken Glass") resulted in the Nazis burning and smashing 7,000 businesses, homes, and Jewish synagogues. Over 30,000 people were sent to concentration camps

1939   *September 1*: Germany invaded Poland

September 3: Britain and France declared war on Germany; later to be joined by Russia

1940   *May 10*: the Germans invaded the Netherlands and established laws against the Jewish population. Anne and Margot now had to attend a Jewish school

1941   *January 8*: Dutch Jews were forbidden to visit theaters, Anne's favorite pastime. They are also prohibited from using public transport

April: the Nazis stated that all Dutch Jews had to wear yellow stars

December 11: USA declared war on Germany. The Allied states fighting the Germans now included Britain, France, Russia, and the USA

1942   *June 12*: Anne received a diary for her thirteenth birthday present

July 5: Margot received orders to be deported to a labor camp. The concentration camps in the Netherlands were at Amersfoort, Ommen, Vught and Westerbork

July 6: the Franks decided to hide in the secret annex to the rear of Otto's office building

1943   *February*: the Germany Army suffered a major defeat at the Battle of Stalingrad and the war began to turn in favor of the Allies

1944   *August 1*: Anne wrote in her diary for the final time

August 4: the inhabitants of the secret annex were betrayed, arrested, and taken to Westerbork camp

September 3: the Franks were transported in freight trains to the concentration camp of Auschwitz in Poland

October 28: Anne and Margot were taken to the Bergen-Belsen concentration camp in Germany

1945   *January 6*: Anne's mother, Edith, died of starvation in Auschwitz

January 27: Auschwitz was liberated by Russian forces. Otto was the sole survivor from the secret annex

March: Margot died of typhus in Bergen-Belsen

April 15: Anne died of typhus in Bergen-Belsen, just days before the camp was liberated by the British Army

April 30: Hitler killed himself rather than risk being captured

May 8: Germany surrendered and the war in Europe ended

June 3: Otto Frank returned to Amsterdam

October 24: Otto received news of the death of his daughters. The faithful Miep Gies gave him Anne's diary that she found in the annex after the family's capture

1952   *June 16*: Anne's diary was published in English as *The Diary of a Young Girl*

For more information about Anne and the secret annex, visit www.annefrank.org

Lightning Source UK Ltd.
Milton Keynes UK
UKHW021355260121
377640UK00002B/88

9 781910 146262